Now It Is
SUMMER

For the Bauers of Chautauqua:
Todd and Susan, Samantha and Emily
— *E. S.*

For Asher and Arianna
— *M. N. D.*

Text © 2011 Eileen Spinelli
Illustrations © 2011 Mary Newell DePalma

Published 2011 by Eerdmans Books for Young Readers
An imprint of Wm. B. Eerdmans Publishing Company
2140 Oak Industrial Dr. NE, Grand Rapids, Michigan 49505
P.O. Box 163, Cambridge CB3 9PU U.K.

Manufactured at Tien Wah Press in Singapore
October 2010, first printing

17 16 15 14 13 12 11   7 6 5 4 3 2 1

Library of Congress Cataloging-in-Publication Data

Spinelli, Eileen.
Now it is summer / by Eileen Spinelli;
illustrated by Mary Newell DePalma.
p. cm.
Summary: A young mouse is encouraged by his mother
to enjoy summer while waiting for autumn to come.
ISBN 978-0-8028-5340-0 (alk. paper)
[1. Mice — Fiction. 2. Summer — Fiction.
3. Autumn — Fiction.]
I. DePalma, Mary Newell, ill. II. Title.
PZ7.S7566Nns 2011
[E] — dc22
          2010017729

The illustrations were rendered
in acrylic paint on watercolor paper.
The display type was set in Kepler and Georgia.
The text type was set in Georgia.

Now It Is
SUMMER

Written by **Eileen Spinelli**

Illustrated by **Mary Newell DePalma**

Eerdmans Books for Young Readers

Grand Rapids, Michigan • Cambridge, U.K.

Will it be autumn soon?
Will a leafy breeze waken me
by ruffling the curtains at my window?
Will it dapple the air with apple-y scent?
Soon?

Yes, it will be autumn soon enough,
but now it is summer.
Now the sun is lemony bright
and the air is spattered sweet
with grass cuttings.
Take a deep breath.

Will it be autumn soon?
Will there be warm cinnamon muffins
on my breakfast plate —
muffins I helped bake?
Soon?

Yes, it will be autumn soon enough,
but now it is summer.
Now there are fresh peaches on your plate.
Remember we found them yesterday
at Old Country Orchard?
Aren't they tasty?

Will it be autumn soon?
Will we make my Halloween costume?
I think I'd like to be a moppy lion this year
or a floppy scarecrow.

Yes, autumn will come
and we will make a lion suit
or scarecrow overalls.
But now it is summer.
Now we need flip-flops
and beach robes
and ice pops from the freezer.
Which flavor would you like?

Will it be autumn soon?
Will the yellow school bus
toot on its route to our house
with all my friends waving at me?
Soon?

Yes, the yellow bus will
beep, beep, beep down our street
in autumn.
But now it is summer.
Now the ferry is waiting.
We'll cross the bay
with your cousins for a picnic.
You can carry the red-checkered tablecloth.
Hurry! The ferry is leaving.

Will it be autumn soon?
Will I leap laughing into leaves
heaped high in the backyard?
Soon?

Yes, autumn will come,
but now it is summer.
Now you can tippy-toe
into the gurgling surf.
Happy splashing!

Will it be autumn soon?
Will I get to choose my pumpkin
from the farmer's patch?
Will I carve a smiling jack-o'-lantern?
Soon?

Yes, it will be autumn
and your jack-o'-lantern will grin and glow.
But now it is summer.
There are soap bubbles to blow
and a beach ball to bounce
across the sand.
Catch it before it bounces
into the ocean!

Will it be autumn soon?
Will we toast marshmallows
around a cozy fire?
And tell shivery stories long past bedtime?
Soon?

Yes, there will be stories and autumn treats
by the fire soon enough.

But now it is summer.
Now there is cold lemonade.
And Grandpa is reading aloud on the porch —
your favorite book.

Will it be autumn soon?
Will the moon rise plump
and orange and high
in a spidery black sky?
Soon?

Yes, there will be an autumn-y orange moon.
But now it is summer.
Now night comes late and the moonlight
is thin as lace
with tiny stars surrounding it.
Make a wish!

Will it be autumn soon?
Will it?

Yes, yes, dear child,
soon enough it will be autumn.
But now it is summer.
Come, take my hand.
Let's go barefoot down the stairs
and out into the shimmery, summery night.
The fireflies are dancing.
Let's join them —
you and me together . . .
joyful . . .
now.

Now!